Voices of Identity

A First Nations Anthology

Lisa Fuller

André Ngāpō

Wilson and Charlene Bearhead

Contents

About the Authors

Lisa Fuller is an award-winning Murri writer living in Canberra with her family. She is a new mum doing her PhD and juggling writing and life.

Lisa says: The topic of **"Political Days"** is important to me, as I often felt very alone and invisible at school when I was growing up. Australia Day is a good example of when First Nations Australians are made to feel excluded, as the day celebrates one of great pain for us. With education and kindness, we can make Australia better for everyone – it's up to each of us to listen and learn. But if someone chooses not to listen, that's not your responsibility or your fault. You can only do your best.

André Ngāpō is an award-winning writer who loves to write stories about his country, Aotearoa New Zealand, and his Māori culture. His Māori ancestors link to Ngāti Porou, Ngāti Awa, Ngāpuhi and Ngāti Tamaterā iwi (peoples).

André says: The setting and themes of **"Kalyn and Taika"** are important to me. I know many children who have moved schools and even countries, and I have seen how much of a culture shock this can be – and how kindness and connection, including back to your whakapapa or ancestral roots, can make all the difference. And as a musician, I know first-hand the joy, solace and power that music can bring to the mind, body and spirit.

Wilson and Charlene Bearhead reside in Treaty 6 territory in what is commonly referred to as Central Alberta, Canada, where they raised six children together. Wilson is Nakota and has been a Chief in his community, a traditional helper in ceremony, and is now an Elder sharing Nakota knowledge and teachings in schools. Charlene is non-Indigenous, an educator and education activist working in pursuit of authentic reconciliation in education across Canada.

Wilson and Charlene say: The setting of **"We Sing the Circle Forward, We Sing the Circle Back"** is deeply personal, reflecting many of the emotions and experiences we have shared while raising our own children, and now teaching our grandchildren.

Political Days

Lisa Fuller

Collapsing on my bed, I stare up at the ceiling and ponder just how messed up things can get in a day. First day back at school in ages, thanks to a worldwide pandemic. I'd been so excited, and a little terrified. Right up until social studies.

Flipping over onto my stomach, I grab my pillow and hug it close. I'd fretted all weekend about my hair, and my clothes. Would I be acceptable? None of it mattered when I walked into class at school. It felt like we'd been separated by screens for so long, no one even looked at or talked about what others were doing. Just too glad to see each other, I guess.

I sat, ready for the last subject of the day, feeling happy and a little buzzed from being able to talk and interact away from my desk at home. My teacher, Mr Klein, is new to the school. His classroom is like any other. White walls, whiteboards, brown desks and chairs. Nothing especially stood out. Most of the classrooms today felt exactly like this. Maybe now that school was back face-to-face, Mr Klein would slowly start filling up the walls with projects, topics and colour.

We spread out to our desks, mine off to the side and not too near the front or the back. Because me and my friends weren't cool enough to sit at the back, and no one liked the front. Not that it bothers me, I've never liked going to the back of anything. Mum and Dad tell me and my brother all those stories about being forced there – Blaks to the Back – on buses, in picture theatres (as Mum and Dad call them) or any other public place. They had no choice, but we do now, and I refuse to ever put myself where others once forced us.

Mr Klein did the usual first day introductions, telling us more about himself and how the subject would go down. No rumours were going around about him, so he likely wasn't a tyrant, but not a favourite either. Then he outlined our assignments for the term.

"I'm going to expect you all to hit the ground running." He clapped his hands together as he stepped between the desks. "Your first assignment is an oral presentation and it's due by the end of the month."

Groans spread throughout the room, and he chortled, walking amongst us. "Don't worry, it's not that hard. It's more about getting to know you. I'd like you to talk about Australia Day, and what it means to you."

He stopped beside me, his eyes darting down for a moment. I saw him register my darker skin, the curly hair. With a flick of his eyes, I became different, other. To him.

He cleared his throat, his eyes shifting away. "Of course, I don't want this to get too political. I want to know about your personal experiences, how it relates to you and your family, how you celebrate the day, that sort of thing. Give me your social and cultural perspectives. I'll be randomly assigning your times to present, so make sure you're prepared."

Walking back to his desk, he never once looked in my direction again. I spent the rest of class watching him not seeing me. This burning sensation started in my chest, making me want to tap my heel on the floor, shaking my leg constantly.

Or maybe jump up and sprint around the oval a few times to burn it away.

The weight of it stayed on the bus ride home, making me clumsy and unfocused. There was no happy buzz, as I stepped down the bus steps and went home.

Trudging into the house, I walked into the kitchen, dumping my bag on the floor as I hunted for chocolate. Mum always had something stashed.

Speaking of, I could hear her coming in now. "Tayah, don't leave the door open like that," she scolded from the door. I heard it shut but just rolled my eyes, still intent on a sugar fix.

"Ah, Mum, chill out," I called back.

I heard a huff, but she was coming closer now. "How was the first day of school? Are you all set with your assignments?"

I tried not to let her pressure hit my shoulders, but it always seems to find its way there. There! My favourite chocolate biscuits. Score!

"Yep," I said, pulling out two biscuits from the packet as Mum rounded the corner into the kitchen.

"Good, anything that you need help –" Mum yelped, and I came out of the pantry cupboard to find her picking up my bag. That she'd just tripped over. "Tayah, you're too old for this. I nearly broke my neck!"

All that dark heaviness inside me bubbled up, like her anger was a match to its oily blackness.

"It was one second," I snapped back. "Maybe look where you're going."

Silence reigned as our equally angry gazes clashed.

"What did you just say to me?" She whispered it in a dangerous tone I rarely hear, but my brother gets a lot.

A small slice of guilt tried to work its way out of my mouth, but I shoved it back.

"I literally just put it there. I'll grab a snack and get straight to my homework."

I didn't even pause to make the cup of tea I'd been planning. I snatched my bag from her hands and stomped towards my room. Every step felt like I was going to get cut down any minute by her scathing tongue.

Somehow, I made it into the hall without Mum saying a word. Not even calling me back. I slammed my bedroom door shut, the anger still buzzing away. But it was mingling with that splash of guilt, and a lot of shock that I'd gotten away with speaking to her like that. I cringed at the thought of what would happen once *her* shock wore off.

Now here I lie. Questioning myself because no one else seemed as affected by the assignment as I was. None of my friends said anything about how Mr Klein had looked at me. Had I even seen it? Maybe it was just me making it up in my head?

Sitting up, I yank my bag to me and rummage for my laptop. Mum and Dad were so proud when I got my scholarship to this posh inner-city school. They went out and splurged, certain I'd need the tech to keep up with my classes. Its silver and black case is a daily reminder of their hopes. Their expectations.

I try to shake off the pressure, like I always do, but this time it sticks like superglue, rubbing against the inside of my skull.

Opening the class webpage, I don't need to dig for the assignment sheet. It's first up, right on top. My first assignment, and the list of who is presenting when. My name is at the top, down to present next week. Guess that gives me no choice.

I go over the sheet again and again. *"Australia Day" – perspectives, celebration, interactions.* Yeah, right. My family don't even go out on that day, Mum had too many bad experiences, so we just stay home. How do you explain parental trauma and protectiveness? You don't.

And what does it mean for me to talk about this anyway? Usually, I'd sit and listen to my family, not lecture others on it.

I stay there a long while, laptop perched on my pillow. Reading over the project again and again. The comment from Mr Klein that sits just above it – *Note: This is not a political debate, so please do not raise any such issues. Think of it as a personal exploration of your family traditions.*

High marks are the only way I keep the scholarship. Anything below a *B* is completely unacceptable to the school, but Mum and Dad made it clear they wanted all *A*s. I picture their faces if I dare bring home anything less ... and cringe. Yeah, that can't happen.

Flipping open a new document on my laptop, I start typing. All the "right" words. The ones Mr Klein made clear he wanted to hear after talking about all his family's traditions. A national pride that I've never felt me and my family were included in. I try to take his words, twist and twirl them to suit my own. But I can't. How to translate those experiences into – that's the day it started, when so many of us would die. To the point where it didn't feel safe for my family to leave the house now.

We spent the day like we always do – each in our rooms, reading or playing games. Dad watching movies or puttering in the backyard.

Nan sat on the back deck all day, drinking an endless supply of tea. Sometimes, she'd tell stories of the many Australia Days in her life. Other times she kept still and silent. No one bothered her when she was like that.

And despite all that, here I sit making up cheery stuff about barbecues and friends. Something to match the life of the teacher, who probably never spent a day in our shoes. The churning inside me is back, darker than ever. And now it's spiked, so it feels like a bad stomach ache. Every word I write sends more sharp stabbing sensations, till I realise the screen has become blurred by the tears.

I shove the laptop and pillow away from me. Wishing I could do the same with this stupid assignment. Grabbing my phone, I'm just about to get my earphones and set off some music. A tap on the door stops me.

It doesn't sound angry.

I so don't want to face this music.

"Yeah?" I call, fighting my inner coward.

"Can I come in?"

It's hard to tell from Mum's voice just how much trouble I'm in.

"Yeah." I still fiddle with my bag, pulling out my headphones as the door opens and shuts.

Her weight lowers onto the side of the bed closest to me, and I finally have to look up. The concern in her eyes pushes my tears back to the fore, but I'm not sure why.

"I'm sorry for snapping at you," she offers.

"Me too," I try to say normally, but it comes out on a choke.

"Daughter, have you been crying?" She reaches out and rubs at the tear that sneaks down my cheek. "Did you have a bad day?"

I shake my head. Nod. Shake.

I don't know how to say this. The darkness inside churns harder, reaching up my throat. If I open my mouth, it'll pour out and I'll have to explain. Then all the tears will escape. And she'll probably tell me I'm being silly. To just write the assignment, present and get my *A*. Who cares about what some teacher thinks about how we experience Australia Day?

She takes one of my hands in hers and sits with me. Waiting for me to work out how or what to say.

If anything. But I can't get my mouth to open, or words to form. So instead, I pick up the laptop and hold it out to her.

Confused, she reaches for it, her eyes seeing immediately that "friendly" comment at the top of the project sheet. As she scrolls down the page and reads more, a slow dawning descends on her.

"Have you already tried to write this?" she asks.

I nod, and wave at her, indicating she can open my document. I can't look at her while she reads it.

She sighs. And that stomach ache inside me intensifies.

"Oh, baby." Her words are sad, but are free of the disappointment I expected.

I finally face her and she's smiling in a soft way. "Can I tell you a story?"

I nod again. This time she waves at me to shuffle over. As I do, she slides up onto the bed with me, using my pillows as a support so she can wrap an arm around me.

"Did I ever tell you about the assignments I wrote in high school?"

"No," I'm able to mutter.

"They were all about Captain Cook and the brave explorers who 'discovered' all the parts of

Australia." I flick her a frown and she twists her lips into a wry smile. "They taught us all about how they found this land, empty and free. Once in a blue moon they'd talk about the savages these intrepid men met on their journeys."

I go rigid and she rubs my shoulder. "I got really good grades for those assignments, too. And I was so proud of myself. It wasn't until I was older that I realised who those savages were. And I've been so ashamed of myself for writing them ever since."

"But they ... I mean, it's not your fault. That's what they taught you," I insist.

She nods, rubbing her fingers through my hair. "True. I didn't know it then. Just like I didn't understand why your grandparents would never come to the school on parent–teacher nights. Or why they put all the Blak kids in the low classes. But I do now. Your school might not be like that, but every generation fights its own battles, and carries its own scars."

She cups my chin and lifts my face until my eyes meet hers. "I know we put a lot on you about keeping your scholarship, but Tayah, no assignment, no grade, is worth that shame I carry. I don't *ever* want you to feel that way."

Her words shine light on the churning dark inside me. I see the raw pain and shame for what it is. The generations of hurt that I carry in me. The hurt that has gone unseen and is still so easily disregarded. I lean into her shoulder in a way I haven't done in a while. We stay like that, with her rubbing my hair, and I feel calmer. Her touch and understanding soothe it. Help. But ...

"What am I going to do about the assignment, though?" I ask, my voice finally sounding normal.

She drops a peck on my forehead. "Let's go talk to Nan."

Hopping up, she walks out, calling for me to bring my laptop. As I walk out to the kitchen, she's on the phone with someone. Based on the nagging, I think it's probably Aunty Kris, Mum's big sister.

"Get the tea on, granddaughter," Nan calls from the back deck. "Make a pot for us all."

By the time the kettle's boiled, Mum, Nan and Aunty Kris are settled outside with my laptop. They're talking but I feel my insides churning again. This time with nerves. I don't want any of them to see what I tried to write. Surely Mum wouldn't show them that.

I run mugs, milk and sugar out to them while they read. No one has said much.

As I head out the back with the fresh pot of tea and the rest of the chocolate biscuits, Mum waves me into the seat next to Nan.

"All right, daughter, let's talk this out."

Stepping into the classroom, I feel the nerves working up my heels again. The urge to tap, tap, tap is so strong. We worked on the assignment for a week, and I have no idea how it's going to go down. Monday, last subject. Mr Klein stands at the front, close to the door as we file in. His eyes dance over me and I feel his anxiety reach out to mine. Still, he offers me a smile.

"Hey, Tayah, all set for your presentation?"

"Sure thing, Mr Klein. Can I go first?"

He looks a bit surprised, but nods. "Great. Thanks for volunteering."

He settles everyone down as I stand to the side.

"All right, everyone, Tayah is first up with her presentation about Australia Day. Before we kick off, just a reminder, this isn't about politics. The class is all about societies, so I want to know your traditions, your family, how you celebrate."

Everyone nods and I stand, working my way to the front. My heart feels like it's trying to break out of my chest and make a run for it. I can feel it pulsing in my fingertips. Mr Klein moves off to one side, leaving the front of the class to me.

I clear my throat, my fingers flicking the note cards in my hand. I stare down at the words I wrote, though, and now I can't mutter them or rush them out.

Taking a few deep breaths, I lower my shoulders, lift my head and open my mouth wide.

"My name is Tayah Harris. I am a Murri one from south-east Queensland, descended from a long line of strong, proud Blak women and men." I can see Mr Klein getting twitchy, like he wants to interrupt. "Australia Day isn't about politics to my family or to anyone in my mob. It's a day of mourning and grief because it's the day the killing started."

There's a soft tap on the classroom door. I flick my eyes to Mr Klein. "This assignment is all about traditions, my society at home. Well, to do it proper way, it's not me you should be talking to. Mr Klein, with your permission ..."

He nods, unsure what I'm asking but not telling me to be quiet. Walking to the door, I open it to find Nan standing there with Aunty Kris, both of them smiling. I give them both a hug and kiss, cos that's how we do things. Even if I only saw Nan this morning. I step back and lead them to the front of the class.

"When we want to learn, we listen to our old people. Our Elders carry knowledge that I can never explain the way they can. This is my grandmother, Mrs Grace Lowell, and my Aunty Kris. Nan's going to show you how we learn through story and listening."

Nan's face turns to the teacher a welcoming smile. "Well, first, can we go outside and sit on the grass in a circle?"

Mr Klein looks a little shocked. "I'm ... umm ... do you have permission to be here?"

Nan pulls a piece of paper from her handbag and hands it to him. "Sorry about that. This is signed by the principal."

Mr Klein reads it over, and eventually nods.

"Umm, okay, I don't see why not. But umm, there is only fifteen minutes and then we've got to be back in class."

"No worries, I'm sure everyone can move faster than me to find the best place to sit," Nan says, smiling all the way as she leads us all to the door.

I wave my friends to join me so we can lead Nan and Aunty outside. Luckily, the classroom opens into a courtyard with a big gum tree close by that throws great shade. I help Nan settle down at the base of the tree and take my spot to one side, waving my class to do the same. Once we're all settled, Nan smiles, spreading her hands out, her palms facing down.

"First, I wish to acknowledge the traditional custodians of this land we're meeting on. I pay my respects to their Elders, past and present. I acknowledge their ongoing care for and connection to Country. This is an important part of our culture for many reasons, but I'll explain that another day if your teacher likes."

She places a palm on my knee and squeezes. "My granddaughter tells me you want to know about what Australia Day means to us. Some people think First Nations peoples are angry about it, that somehow not liking the day means we hate Australia. That's not true at all. We're hurting and sad, because that day in 1788 means nothing but pain for our peoples. The fact that Australia Day is set there now – which it wasn't always – means we can't celebrate with everyone else. And that feels like one more way we're excluded from the nation."

Lying on my bed staring at the ceiling, I keep wondering if I've failed the assignment. A big part of me doesn't care, because Nan was so deadly today and I loved every second of it. All the other students came up after to thank her, and to tell me how cool it was. Mr Klein let us go for a lot longer than those fifteen minutes, too, but some of the others still complained when he said we had to go back cos other people still had to present.

Still, as I walked out, he was staring at me with the weirdest look in his eyes. Aunty Kris drove us home, her and Nan yarning the whole way. Mum had wanted to be there, but she had a big meeting on this afternoon. Aunty Kris had texted her updates. But now I have a lot of time to flip that look from Mr Klein around in my head. I still have no idea what it means.

A tap on the door. "Tayah, can I come in?" Mum calls out.

"Yeah," I say, sitting up on my elbows to look at her.

Standing in the open doorway, she gives me a huge smile, her eyes sparkling and so much joy in them. "I heard it went great. Come on, we're going out to celebrate."

I frown at her. "But ... I still don't have my mark. What if I've failed? What are we even celebrating then?" The anxiety I've been trying to ignore since we hatched this plan over the week has been plaguing me. I've been fighting it, but not very successfully.

Shaking her head in amusement, she walks into the room. Holding her hand out to me, she waits till I take it so she can pull me up to stand before her. She places her hands on my shoulders, staring into my face, making sure I'm listening.

"A mark on some assignment doesn't mean anything in the grand scheme of things. Hopefully, your teacher was listening and learning today. I'm sure Nan did her best. But others' learning is not in your control, and neither is how they react to things. What we can control is how *we* choose to behave.

Which is why we're celebrating your bravery tonight, daughter. For standing up and doing the hard thing, even when others made it feel like you couldn't, or that you shouldn't. And doing it in a kind, open-hearted way that hopefully helps others learn and understand. We're so proud of you."

I feel the tears threatening again, and she knows I hate to cry. Because I'm just like her. She pulls me in for a hug and we're both laughing through a few tears.

"Come on now, grab a coat. And think about where you want to go," she says as she walks out the door, leaving me to do just that.

Coat on in seconds, I'm halfway out the door when my laptop buzzes with a sound I know well and usually has me running to check it. Assignment marked.

I feel the normal pull to check my grade, but the sound of women laughing calls me to them. Carefully, I close the door and walk away. It can wait. Some things are more important.

Kalyn and Taika

André Ngāpō

Māori Words

āe – yes
aroha ki te tangata – love to each person
haka – a form of singing and dancing
hongi – to press noses in greeting
ka rawe – excellent
kaea – the leader of a kapa haka group
kai – food/meal/to eat
kapa haka – a Māori performing group
kia ora – hello
manu – bird
Nau mai, haere mai – welcome
pōhiri – welcoming ceremony
poi – a light ball on a string which is swung or twirled to sung accompaniment
pounamu – greenstone
Te Matatini – a large kapa haka competition
te reo Māori – the Māori language
tika – correct
waiata – song/singing
whānau – family
whānau Māori – Māori family

Kalyn and Taika

Kalyn

Monday, 8:37 am

Beeeeep! A car horn from behind makes us all jump out of our skins.

"Oops," says Mum. "I'm blocking the lane. This school traffic is pretty busy!"

Mum is just getting used to driving in the city. We've only been here a week. Today is our first day at our new school.

"City drivers are impatient," says my little brother, Teo. Another car honks its horn loudly, and Teo rolls his eyes with a smile. "See!" he says.

I'd rather walk to school, like we did back home. But we can't. At our old school, Te Kura, we would cut through farm paddocks and make it from home to school in ten minutes. Some of the kids at Te Kura would come to school on a horse. But here, if we walked we'd have to cross a busy motorway.

Mum pulls into a parking space as dozens of kids stream past us.

"Here we are: Berkshire Intermediate," says Mum. She gets out of the car with us and checks that we have everything. "Good luck with finding those nice boys you met at the open day."

We visited Berkshire last term for a school tour before we moved to the city. Just like us, quite a few other kids were moving schools part-way through the year. Now here we are, ready to start Term 2.

Berkshire is a lot different from my last school. At Te Kura, there were only twenty-seven kids, and all of our younger siblings went there, too. Because Berkshire is an intermediate, all eight hundred kids are the same ages as Teo and me.

"Oh, and Kalyn, before I forget," says Mum, looking my way, "you make sure you watch out for Teo on his first day at intermediate school." Teo and I both chuckle. He's bigger and taller than me, even though he's only eleven and I'm twelve. I'm faster, though.

"I'll keep an eye on him." I smile and Teo smiles back.

"Lucky me!" he says with a laugh.

"And remember to enjoy yourselves," Mum says. "I'm sure you'll both have lots of new friends by the end of the day."

I hope so, too.

Approaching the school gates, I feel a bit strange. This is so different to Te Kura. Back there, the new kids joining our school would wait with their families at the gates before being welcomed in properly with a *pōhiri*. We would do speeches, sing *waiata* and do the *haka*, and press our noses together in the *hongi* to say they were now one of our school family – our *whānau*. And last but not least, we would share a yummy *kai* together.

Here at Berkshire, it is like the whole school is trying to rush through the gate all at once, a few adults included. It's busier than a chicken coop at feeding time! And there's no welcoming ceremony or anything. Someone decides to turn the situation into a game, with some of the bigger boys bouncing around like pinballs. And as I get carried along with the crowd, I feel my sandal go *crunch* on something soft. I've stood on someone's foot.

"Ahhh!" I hear someone yell. But before I can say sorry, they are swallowed up by the jumble of bodies, and I can only make out the lime green colour of the bag on their back as an adult leads them quickly to the office.

Finally, Teo and I make it into the main courtyard, just in time for the big assembly.

Riiiiiiiiing.

The bell cuts through the excited chatter, and when it finishes, everyone is twice as loud as before. The teachers come and usher the students into their class groups, with the new kids heading towards the class teacher they met at the open day. Some of the kids I met before wave and smile. My year group sits on one side, and Teo's on the other.

"Hey!" whispers a boy from the class line next to ours, waving to me. I recognise him from the open day.

"Hi, Manawa," I say.

"You remembered!" he says. "Kalyn, right?"

I only have time to nod. The assembly has begun.

There is a silence as the principal, Mrs Flegler, raises her hand. I notice that it looks like she is pointing towards a *manu* soaring high in the sky. There are hardly any trees here compared to back in the country. I'm amazed that there are any manu living in the city at all.

"*Kia ora*, Berkshire Intermediate," she says, "and welcome back to another exciting school term." There are a few snickers. Some of the teachers ask for quiet, and everyone quickly settles. As Mrs Flegler talks, I can't help but wonder if Manawa and the other new kids are as nervous as I am about their first day at Berkshire.

I think about the pōhiri back at Te Kura. The speeches must be nearly done there. Soon, they'll all be digging into the kai. My stomach rumbles, even though it's not that long since I had breakfast! Manawa looks over from his line and pats his stomach, as if the noise came from him. We both smile.

Once the assembly is finished, my new class and I thread our way through the maze of buildings and up several flights of stairs to Room 32. I have to laugh – Te Kura only had one big room, with a divider wall in between that we could open up when needed. Berkshire is absolutely huge!

I hang my bag on a hook that has the label I made at the open day, then sit with the others in a circle on the grey carpet. Mrs Loft sits on the floor with us, too. My old teacher, Matua Jim, used to sit on the floor with us at Te Kura.

Mrs Loft looks towards the class.

"Right, Room 32," she says. "I would like us all to spend some time introducing ourselves to Kalyn again." Ravi starts, and we have nearly made it the whole way around the circle when there is a knock at the door.

"Miss," says Penelope to Mrs Loft, "it's Mrs Flegler."

The principal opens the door, and when she steps into the class there is a boy standing beside her. His hair is almost completely covering his face.

"Sorry to interrupt, Mrs Loft," says Mrs Flegler. "The new student I discussed at the staff meeting has arrived, and I felt your class would be the best fit. Everyone, this is Taika. He will be joining Room 32."

"Welcome, Taika," says Mrs Loft in her kind voice. "That's great timing. We are just doing our introductions as a class. Kalyn here is also new to the school."

I see Taika look out from under his hair, and when his eyes catch mine I am sure he glares at me.

"Taika, please pop your bag outside on a spare hook, and then come and sit next to me."

As he turns, I see a lime green bag and recognise it. It was his foot I stood on this morning.

That's why he glared at me! And when he sits down, I know he is upset about it. He looks straight at me and his eyes narrow.

Taika

Monday, 6:37 am

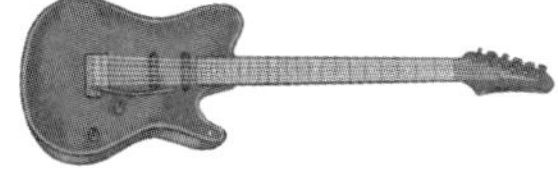

As my eyes open, it takes me a few seconds to remember where I am. This is not my bed, not my pillow, and these are not my blankets. The walls are a different colour, and the windows are on the wrong side. The noises are completely different here – I can barely make out the singing of the birds over the motorway traffic.

I sit up and the blur of the last few days comes back to me. I'm at Uncle's and Auntie's new house in Auckland. On Friday night, we hurriedly packed some travel bags and raced up to be with my little brother, Bodie. He's in Starship Hospital – he had to fly there in a helicopter ambulance because he couldn't breathe properly. The doctors say it could be a few months before he can go home, and until then we will stay at Uncle's and Auntie's. Mum is up at the hospital with him right now.

As much as I am worried about Bodie, I didn't want to come to Auckland, and I asked if I could stay back in Wellington at my nanna's house – I want to keep going to my old school. Our family only moved to New Zealand from Australia at the start of the year, and I don't want to change schools again. At first it was embarrassing explaining my Australian accent to everyone. And with my *pounamu* and brown skin, some of them had teased me for being a wannabe. But I managed to make some friends there. I was even part of a school band – I play guitar. We were supposed to have a big performance this term. I didn't even have time to take my guitar before we left. And Uncle and Aunty don't play.

But Mum and Dad said I had to come to Auckland. It would be too much for Nanna, who is already looking after my little cousins. "Whānau sticks together, that's our family motto," Dad said.

Mum agreed. "Dad already works from home, and you can go to school up here so we can all stay together."

I can hear Dad now, out in the kitchen talking to Uncle in *te reo Māori*. When they speak in the Māori language, they sound exactly the same and I can't tell them apart. Dad hardly ever speaks Māori at home, because Mum is Australian. Dad and Uncle are laughing a lot, too – more like giggling – trying not to wake anyone up, but doing a terrible job of it.

I lie under the covers for ages, even when the smell of breakfast slips under the crack of the door and tries to tempt me out of bed. I don't feel hungry. I don't want to go to school today. Mum and Dad said I needed to go to Berkshire Intermediate, where my cousin Leroy used to go. Aunty has even dug out his old uniform that they hadn't yet got around to taking to the second-hand store.

"You'll only have to go there for this term, maybe a little more," Mum said. But I'd rather go up to the hospital and be with the family, even if hospitals are boring.

"We need you to go to school, Taika, so we can take care of your brother," said Dad.

"What about our family motto?" I asked.

Dad put his hand on my shoulder and smiled at me.

"Going to school is the best way to help the whānau right now, Taika," he said. "It's your last year before high school. We don't want you to get too far behind. And you're already better than me at spelling and maths – I won't be able to teach you a thing." Dad was joking, but I couldn't even force a smile. I felt too annoyed.

Uncle says he will drop me off to my first day at Berkshire this morning, so Dad can go to a meeting with the specialist doctors at the hospital. As we make our way through the thick traffic, Uncle tells me how much Leroy loved his time at Berkshire. As he tells me about it, I have to admit it sounds just like my school in Wellington. And as we slowly edge towards the school carpark, I can see it looks really similar, too – the same style of building, and it's even painted the same colours. I can't help but wonder if the same people built both schools. Then I see the swarms of kids, and I remember I don't know anybody here. And to make things worse, I'm wearing Leroy's faded old uniform that's too big for me.

"Car parking is really hard here sometimes," says Uncle as a horn toots in front of us. "Looks like there's a car up there blocking the road."

A horn blares loudly from behind us.

"Hold ya horses," says Uncle. "These city drivers are always in such a rush."

Finally, the car blocking the road moves, and before we know it, we are walking towards the school gates. Uncle says he'll talk with the office staff, as he only rang them this morning to see if it was okay for me to start. He needs to fill in the forms with my details.

"Luckily they said it was okay for you to start today on such short notice."

Not very lucky at all, I think to myself.

We head towards the entrance, but we can see there is construction work happening and the main gates are closed, so everyone is having to squeeze through a side gate.

Uncle leads me into the loud mass of kids, and he manages to get through with ease. But I get tangled up with a big group playing tag, and some of the kids behind me start to push and shove, laughing and thinking it's funny when it's not.

Suddenly, I feel a sharp pain in my foot

"Ahhh!" I scream. Some kid has stood on it! And to make matters worse, it's like he has a stone lodged into the sole of his shoe. I'm sure I heard him laugh, too.

I catch a glimpse of his face and then try to take a look at my foot, but I can't stop as there are too many kids all surging forward.

"You're bleeding," says Uncle as I hobble over to him. "We better get into the office quick to get that looked at."

While Uncle talks to the secretary and fills out the paperwork, my foot is checked by the school nurse.

"It's a scratch, really," she tells me, "but it sure did bleed! It'll be fine now that I've cleaned it."

The pain is not so bad anymore, but the nurse needed to put on some plasters and tape and my foot feels really uncomfortable, now.

By the time we've finished in the office, the school assembly is already finished. The school principal, Mrs Flegler, introduces herself and says she will take me to join my new class, Room 32. Walking through the school grounds, it's like I could be back in Wellington, it is so similar. But I see a class through the windows, and the colour of their red uniforms reminds me that this place is completely new. I feel like an outsider.

"Here we are," says Mrs Flegler. "Room 32. You will love Mrs Loft and your new classmates. Another boy, Kalyn, has started today, too."

In the classroom, all the kids are sitting in a circle, with the teacher at the front. I keep my head down. It's embarrassing walking in late and having all of their eyes on me.

Mrs Loft welcomes me and says the class is doing introductions. And then I spot him, the boy who stood on my foot and laughed. I hang up my bag and take a seat in the circle.

I look at the other new boy. Mrs Loft said his name was Kayln.

"You wait, Kalyn," I whisper under my breath as I stare into his shocked face. *"You wait."*

Kalyn
Monday, 3:08 pm

"How was your first day, boys?" Dad asks as he picks us up from school.

Teo raves about it all, the different subjects, his new friends, the sports auditorium, and especially the cooking room.

"It was okay," I say, when it's my turn.

The car slowly crawls along in the traffic.

I tell Dad about seeing Manawa again and how we hung out at lunchtime, and about meeting some of the kids from his class.

Then I tell him about Taika, how he ignored me and gave me the evil eye the whole day.

"A new boy, eh?" says Dad.

"Yeah," I say. "And he didn't really talk. He just hid behind his hair. He sounded Australian, but I think he's Māori. His name is Taika."

"Sounds like he was nervous," says Dad. "Just be extra nice to him. That always works for me. *Aroha ki te tangata* – love to each person."

I can't help but smile when Teo, who has been humming along to the rock song on Dad's playlist, says, "You love us, right, Dad? Can you get us an ice cream for getting through our first day at school?"

Dad laughs.

That evening after dinner, I ask if we can watch *Te Matatini* online. Te Matatini is a big *kapa haka* competition. The groups dress up in traditional Māori costumes, and they sing and dance and make speeches. Ever since I can remember, I have wanted to perform at Te Matatini. I want to be a *kaea*, a leader, and make a speech on stage to the thousands of people listening. I want to do my people proud.

“Did Mrs Loft say when the kapa haka group practises, boys?” Dad asks as one group departs the stage.

“Wednesday,” I say to Dad. I feel nervous. I really want to join the school kapa haka group, but what if there is no space for me? Or what if I am not good enough?

Wednesday, 12:48 pm

Wednesday afternoon finally arrives, and as Teo, Manawa and I step into the *whānau Māori* department classroom at lunchtime, I know I don’t need to feel worried. I feel like I have been transported to Te Kura. I can tell by Teo’s face that he feels it, too. Everyone is singing and laughing, there are posters of famous Māori people on the walls and there are guitars everywhere.

The steady beat of *poi* twirling and spinning is like a lullaby as a group of girls practises their latest song.

The teacher spots us and walks over with a big smile.

“*Nau mai, haere mai*,” he says, welcoming us.

He asks us if we would feel comfortable with a formal welcome.

“*Āe, tika* – yes,” I say. Teo nods.

And soon there are speeches, and singing and haka, just like back home. When we sing our waiata, I play guitar at the same time, and soon there are three other kids playing along with me– they know this waiata as well.

Then it is time to hongi all of the other kids, pressing noses together even though it is the first time we have ever met. Teo and I are a part of the family now.

As I glance out the window, I see Taika peering in, but he spins on his heel and walks off when he sees me looking. He hasn't really been mean to me, but he hasn't talked to me once. I think he thinks I stood on his foot on purpose. And if I try to explain, he just quickly walks away. If only he didn't have it in for me.

Taika
Wednesday, 3:27 pm

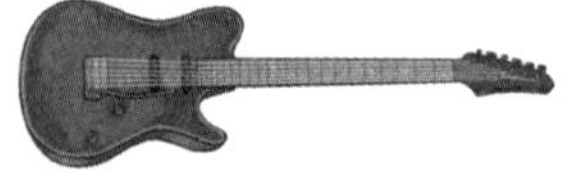

Mum picks me up from school, today. She's spent most of the last six days at the hospital, but today it is Dad's turn. He has a day off work so Mum can chill out a bit. But even though she looks really tired, and Uncle could have picked me up from school, she's still come to pick me up.

Mum grew up in Sydney. She's an expert in city traffic, and she weaves in and out of the school traffic, then steers the car towards the motorway.

"Bodie is doing really well," she says. "The doctors think he will be out by the end of the term."

I feel relieved. I can't wait to get back to Wellington.

Mum asks me about school.

"Tell me about the boy who stood on your foot," she says.

I look at her. How does she know?

"I rang Mrs Loft today to see how you're settling in, and she'd noticed you've been a bit grumpy towards the other new boy, Kalyn. She said that when she asked you about it, you went quiet."

I feel my cheeks become hot.

I tell her about the way he laughed when he stood on my foot and didn't even say sorry. And when Mrs Loft asked me about it, I still felt so mad that I couldn't even get the words out.

"But are you sure it was him?" she says. "Did you ask him about it?"

I stop to think about it. I'm sure it was him. I mean, I'm pretty sure.

"Well," she says. "Remember last week when I thought Dad had eaten the biscuits and left the packet on the bench?"

I nod. It was actually me who did that. It seems like it was a year ago.

"So, it is possible that it may have been someone else. Or he might not have meant to do it. I mean, have you noticed any other times he has been unkind to you or to anyone else?"

"No," I say.

"Mrs Loft says he's a lovely boy. And standing on someone's foot and laughing about it doesn't sound like something someone would do on their first day at a new school."

The more I think about it, the more I think Mum could be right. Kalyn seems like he's probably a nice guy. The kids in the whānau Māori department thought so. I got invited too, but I felt too shy. I just watched from the window.

"Okay, Mum," I say. "I'll try to talk to him about it tomorrow. I think you might actually be right."

"I'm glad," she says, smiling. "And, about getting mad – that's not like you, you're usually so calm.

I think there's been a lot going on for you, Taika. You're probably mad because you've been uprooted all of a sudden and got thrown into a new school. Dad and I are sorry you have had to move twice this year, now. If there was another way, so you didn't have to move, we would have done it."

I feel my eyes get a little hot and turn to look out the window at the passing traffic. I think about Bodie in the hospital – he is going through far worse than me.

"Now," says Mum, wiping her own eyes, "Dad said if you'd been mean to another kid that perhaps you shouldn't get the surprise we'd agreed on yesterday."

Surprise?

"But it sounds like that business with Kalyn is going to be cleared up, and I'm satisfied that when I ring Mrs Loft tomorrow, it'll all be sorted out."

We pull into a shopping mall carpark, a place I've never been before.

"So, I see no reason why you shouldn't get your surprise today. You did save up for it, after all."

My heart skips a beat. There's only one thing I've been saving up for. But surely not today. I won't let myself believe it, just in case I am wrong.

We walk towards the front doors of the mall, and as they open my eyes dart around, searching for confirmation. But all I can see is a barber shop, a café, an electronics shop and some clothes stores.

"So, I know you have your first guitar lesson at school tomorrow," says Mum. "And Dad and I realise your old guitar is back in Wellington."

Yes! I think to myself. I was right!

I signed up for rock guitar lessons, just like I had back in Wellington, and I was going to have to borrow an old school guitar. I know what she is going to say next.

"So, today is the day you get your new guitar. I rang to check, and they have the exact one you want. Happy early birthday, Taika!"

I can't believe it! I've been saving up for a new guitar since we moved to New Zealand. I even have the model picked out, but I thought I'd have to wait a few months yet.

And as we leave the music store, I feel like I'm walking on a cloud.

Kalyn
Thursday, 8:57 am

Making our way through the carpark, Teo and I are spotted by Manawa and some of the kids we met in the whānau Māori room.

"Hey, Kalyn! Teo! Kia ora!" they call. Some of them are playing touch rugby, some of them are practising poi and some of the others are singing and playing guitar. I notice kids from other cultures and countries are joining in, too, and they know the words.

But then I hear Teo say, "Oh-oh." I spin around and see Taika walking straight towards me.

He looks serious. What's his problem? I didn't do it on purpose!

"Kalyn," he says. "I need to talk to you."

"I'm sorry, I didn't stand on your foot on purpose," I blurt out defensively.

Some of the other kids gather around to see what the fuss is all about.

"Yeah," says Taika. "Sorry it took me so long to figure that out. And sorry I gave you the silent treatment."

We take a seat at a picnic table, and he tells me how he was born in Australia and has only been in New Zealand since the start of the year. He tells me about his little brother, and the rare disease the doctors just discovered this week. And he tells us how he had to pack up on the weekend and start at a new school, just like that.

"I've been angry since we left Australia," he says. "You guys are the first people I've ever talked to about it."

Teo and Manawa are there, too, and I can tell that, like me, they feel sorry for Taika. He seems like such a nice guy.

"You should come and hang out with us at morning tea and lunch," says Teo.

I notice his electric guitar case now. We tell him about all the guitars in the whānau Māori room, and how we can teach him some Māori songs.

"I've already been invited to try out for a rock band at lunchtime," he says, smiling. "A kid saw my guitar at the gate, and he said they were looking for a guitarist."

"Can I come and watch?" asks Teo. "I love rock music!"

"Sure," says Taika. "It's in the music room."

"I'll come watch, too," I say. Along with inheriting Mum's love of kapa haka, Teo and I grew up on Dad's rock music. Dad sometimes jokes that I was born to lead a kapa haka group, and Teo was born to be the lead singer in a rock group.

"That sounds cool," says Taika. "And tomorrow I will come to the whānau Māori room. My dad speaks Māori, but not very often, and I want to learn."

"*Ka rawe*!" I say to him. "That means 'excellent'."

"Dad says that one, too," Taika says.

"Ka rawe," we all say at once, and then burst out laughing.

Taika
Thursday, 1:07 pm

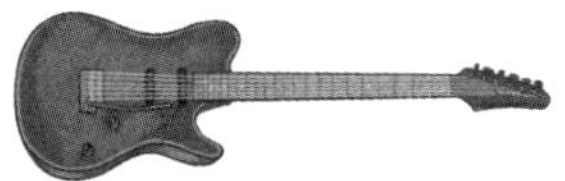

I'm strumming along to the beat. The guitar feels amazing under my fingers, and as much as I love my old guitar back in Wellington, I know that this new guitar was worth every cent I paid for it. It makes playing feel so easy.

The band and I decided on a song we all knew, and from the first bar it was like we'd been playing together for ages. Aidan, the band leader, breaks into a loud drum fill and looks at me to take on the guitar solo. I let rip with a nice series of licks, and as I look up I am surprised to see Mrs Loft standing at the door, nodding her head in time with the music.

When the song draws to a close, there's a round of applause from the kids crammed into the room around us, and from those squashed up against the windows and door.

"Wow! Taika, you're amazing!" says Aidan. I feel a bit embarrassed when kids start coming in and patting me on the back and introducing themselves.

"Now all we need is a lead singer," says Aidan.

I can see Kalyn whispering to Teo, pushing him forward.

"Teo will try out as singer," says Kalyn.

I remember him saying he was really into rock.

And soon, the microphone is out and we're all rocking away. Teo is great!

Everyone laughs when Manawa says he will play the cowbell.

It's time to go back to class, but it takes a while for the buzz to die down. Eventually, Mrs Loft has to ask everyone to go to their classes. Kalyn and I spend the afternoon in Room 32 talking about Australia and his old school, Te Kura, music, and moving away from home. We agree that we will meet up on the weekend if it's okay with our parents.

Walking towards the school gates at the end of the day, I hear some of the kids from the music room calling out goodbye, and I feel happier than I have felt since we moved to New Zealand, back before Christmas.

"How was the day?" Dad asks, as he opens the back door so I can slot my guitar case into the space between the seats.

"Ka rawe," I say, smiling. "It was excellent."

"Oh, ka rawe!" he says, smiling too, as he pulls into the steadily moving traffic.

We Sing the Circle Forward, We Sing the Circle Back

Wilson and Charlene Bearhead

Nakota Words

Ade – my father

chanupta – willow fungus

Ena – my mother

Ena Makoochay – Mother Earth

Michish – my son

mitakuye oyasin – all are related

Mitowjin – my grandson

Mugoshin – my grandmother

Waka – Creator

wasiju – white man

We Sing the Circle Forward, We Sing the Circle Back

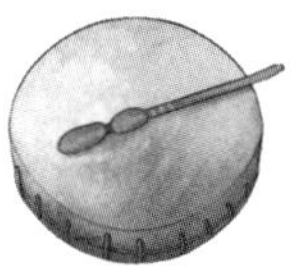

As I sit in this circle, my back curved from years of hard work and ceremony, I see myself in *Mitowjin* – my grandson – sitting across the circle from me. It seems not long ago that I was that young boy.

I remember the day I told *Ade* – my father – that I wanted to sing. I wanted to learn the ceremonies of my people – the Nakota people – the way my father did and my grandfather. I remember how Ade told me that it would be a long road of learning. It would not be easy, but I had a good start because I could speak my language, thanks to my grandmother – *Mugoshin* – Annie.

I still hear her voice in my head, how she'd call on me to saddle up her old mare – Lady – so we could ride to the lake to join the ceremony. Mugoshin would tell me stories of our people – always in our language – as Lady would faithfully plod along the all-too-familiar path.

Now, sitting in the circle, with each beat of the drum I can hear Lady's hooves striking the ground. In the echo of the singers, I hear Mugoshin's words.

Many years have passed since those days, so long ago. Yet it seems only yesterday that my father took me to my uncle to learn the story of the drum.

I was just a boy, the age Mitowjin is now. That was the very first time I heard the story of the drum, and it's etched into the walls of my mind. The responsibilities of the drum keeper, the humility required to carry the songs, each word of each story – all in our Nakota language, all in my uncle's voice – **reverberate** in my memory just as clearly as when he first shared them with me on that cold winter day, so long ago.

As the memories come back to me, flickering in my mind like the flames of the fire burning next to me, I feel the energy of my youth and the memory of my deep desire to be part of these ways flare up in my tired, weathered body.

I watch the drum in Mitowjin's hand, and I feel the energy connecting his drumstick to my drumstick as they strike our hand drums at exactly the same time. I see his lips move, and in his voice I hear my own younger voice come from deep within him ... from deep in his heart. Mitowjin's eyes are closed tight as he focuses on the teachings, the stories and the message of the song that I passed along to him, just as my uncle passed them along to me.

I wonder if Mitowjin hears my words in his mind the way I hear my uncle. I wonder what it is within him that makes him choose these ways when so many of his uncles and cousins chose a different path. No matter what it is, I am grateful to *Waka* – Creator – for giving Mitowjin the spirit that he has, and for the visions that he sees while his eyes are closed tight, and his voice carries his prayers.

My eyes are wide open now ... as I sing with Mitowjin, and with all of the men in our circle. Mixed with humble gratitude to be part of this circle, I have such pride in Mitowjin. He is here for his people, for his family and to take care of his spirit as I've taught him to do.

I have shared the teachings with so many young people, but not all have seen the value. Many of our young people see these ways as outdated. They say our ways are dying and have no value in this world. They are so sadly mistaken and my heart breaks for them, as one day they will realise that the solutions to so many of the challenges that we face all across *Ena Makoochay* – Mother Earth – are carried in our stories. They are the teachings that have helped us to care for all our relations ... the four-legged ones, the winged ones, the crawlers and the swimmers, just as they take care of us: the two-legged. This path is not easy but it's a good road to travel.

Mugoshin Annie offered her teachings to many of her grandchildren as well, but only I carried them in my heart and made them part of my life. Her other grandchildren chose not to take up our ways, to not speak our language, and many of them are lost.

As I watch Mitowjin, his eyes closed tight, embracing the teachings and songs of prayer that I passed on to him, I'm filled with gratitude that he chose to accept the gifts that I could only offer to him, and to carry them to the next generations and beyond. I am so grateful that the fire of my people, the Nakota, my family, my uncle and my grandmother, will live on through him.

The smell of the sweetgrass, the sage and *chanupta* – willow fungus – waft through the air like a familiar, soothing call to my spirit. I'm drawn back to the moment, here in this sacred place, and my eyes make the slow and steady journey around the circle of singers. We all sing the same songs, the songs that we have sung together since we were just young, learning from our fathers, our uncles and our grandfathers – just as they sang these same songs that were passed down to them.

In each face I see stories. I see the wrinkles and crevices of age in my brothers, and the committed **anticipation** in the faces of their sons. In some, I recognise the scars – both on their bodies and on their spirits – that came from the struggles that we have all faced in our lives. The assaults have been many since the arrival of the *wasiju* – white man. When they came to these lands we made space for them, guided them so that they might live well on these lands, as we had always done. We welcomed them in the spirit of *mitakuye oyasin* – we are all related.

Our people believed that there was enough for everyone, that we could share what was provided for the two-legged with these wasiju as well, and there would have been, had the newcomers honoured our non-human relatives in the same way that we do.

How could we have anticipated the greed they would exhibit? How could our ancestors even imagine a way of life where the two-legged could believe themselves to be more powerful than the water, the wind and Ena Makoochay herself? How could we have known that these people, arriving here sick, weak and lost, could turn so quickly to try to destroy everything we knew? Who could have anticipated their fear and hatred of all that we had offered them as a means of living well on these lands, choosing to destroy all traces of it in favour of their own self-serving ways?

Those were, and still are, some very hard things for our people to live through, but the strength in these voices prove that we are here, and we are strong. It's the teachings of our old people, old like I am now, that have carried us to this day in a good way.

The songs lift my spirit and my mind drifts through the memories of what we have come through together – my brothers and me, my parents and my people – over time.

The arthritis pain shooting through my back and hands jolt me back to my time as a young boy, pulling the fish nets out of the holes Ade had drilled into the ice on the frozen lake.

The heavy nets were a good sign because it meant we would have fish for supper that night and Ade could sell the fish to buy the things we needed for *Ena* – my mother – to thicken the soup and make the **bannock** that would fill our stomachs along with the fish soup. But those heavy nets also took a toll on my body over time. The freezing temperatures were not kind to my hands and the strain on my small body left its mark that I still feel today.

The contrasting memories of those bountiful nets and the strain on my physical self-being reflect my reality today. As I sit here, legs crossed on the bony back of Ena Makoochay, Mother Earth, contributing to her heartbeat as my drum blends with all the others, my heart is full while my body aches. But the spirit is strong and today my spirit soars.

As one song ends and another begins, my eyes once again navigate the familiar terrain of the ones I share this life with. Beyond the circle of the men who sing, beyond the keepers of the pipes and the one who sits on the buffalo robe, are the women, the strength of our people, the ones who give us life and who have kept us strong ... like Mugoshin Annie.

With my children I tried my best, despite my many shortfalls, just as my father and his father did before me. The interference by the wasiju fractured our spirits, as they tried to erase our ways.

The women have always had a **revered** place in our communities. It's the women who give life, keep the fire burning and carry half of the knowledge and teachings for every aspect of our lives. Despite the many and intentional violations of our way of life, the women and men came together, just as we do in this ceremony today, to close the circle and do our best to protect what was given to us by Waka. That we sit here together, sharing our stories, our prayers and our songs, affirms that our best was more than good enough.

I know that Mugoshin Annie is with us, just as she appeared to me in the **sweat lodge** all those years ago. She sees the callouses on my hands, and on the hands of *Michish* and Mitowjin, so she knows that her lessons of hard work for a good life live on in us all. The teachings that she shared with me, the lessons that she gifted to me, became the stories that I have shared with my children and grandchildren when times were the most difficult of all.

I watch their hands wrapped tightly around their drumsticks, evidence of the strong ties between her teachings and the ceremony we participate in together here today. Mugoshin Annie's image illuminates my mind, the warmth of her strong but loving words fills my heart as the voices of the singers, including my own, surround me with the reminders of all I have to be grateful for ... most of all, Mitowjin ... we will live on in him.

As I sit in this circle, my back curved from years of hard work and ceremony, I feel the love of Mitowjin, my grandson, as he looks to me and he sings. I see the kindness in his face – a handsome, gentle face with less pain in his eyes than the ones who came before him – and humble pride in his Nakota ways. My heart is full as he sings the circle back around to me.

That he can sing every word in the language first taught to me assures me that I have honoured my teachers – Mugoshin Annie, my father, my uncles. I have done what Waka put me here to do. I am living the life that my mother could only hope that I would live. I've passed this beautiful Nakota language that Waka gifted to me to my children and grandchildren – as it was meant to be. The waves of **oppression** and **assimilation** that flooded our lands and crashed up against us made us stronger swimmers.

I'm proud that Mugoshin Annie's teachings of how kindness and strength must live hand in hand have not been lost or fractured. The tenderness in Mitowjin's face and the power in his voice is proof that our spirits are not broken. The deep love we share for each other confirms that the essence of who we are – who we have always been – is intact and is strong.

As I watch Mitowjin, the voices of the singers lift my spirit and my back hurts a little less. I sit just a little bit straighter. My voice gets a little bit higher, and it carries a little bit further. I know that it's these ceremonies and our Nakota ways that guided me to the path and the life I live today. Our ways and the strong spirits of our people are what made it possible for Michish and Mitowjin to sit in this circle, to participate and connect in all the ways that the newcomers hoped we wouldn't.

It's these ways that taught me to embrace who I am as a Nakota person and live it in every aspect of my life ... to encourage my children and grandchildren to learn and follow our ways ... to make relatives with all peoples with the same respect and honour that we embrace in making relatives with the four-legged, the winged, the plant people and all creation. As Mugoshin Annie always said: "to be a good visitor here on earth".

As the last song comes to a close, and my gaze once again drifts beyond Mitowjin and Michish ... beyond the circle of men drumming ... I see the many and the different sitting in this sacred circle. All different colours, some speaking different languages, sharing the spirit of this sacred place, this ceremony, this connection to Waka that in turn connects us all to one another. There is no pain, no sadness, no loneliness in this place. Only warmth, love, joy, humility and gratitude.

Just as I stand on the shoulders of my ancestors and those who came before me – those who kept this path clear for me – I have the strength to carry my children and grandchildren, all children I've had the honour of teaching, as they learn and prepare to walk this path forward for seven generations and more.

Glossary

anticipation	a feeling of excitement about something that is going to happen
assimilation	the process of being absorbed by another culture, often through the imposition of their customs, language and beliefs
bannock	a type of bread that can be baked or fried
oppression	the exercise of authority or power in cruel and unjust ways
reverberate	to echo or resound
revered	regarded as worthy of great honour and respect
sweat lodge	heated dome-like structures that are used by some Indigenous peoples for religious or medicinal purposes